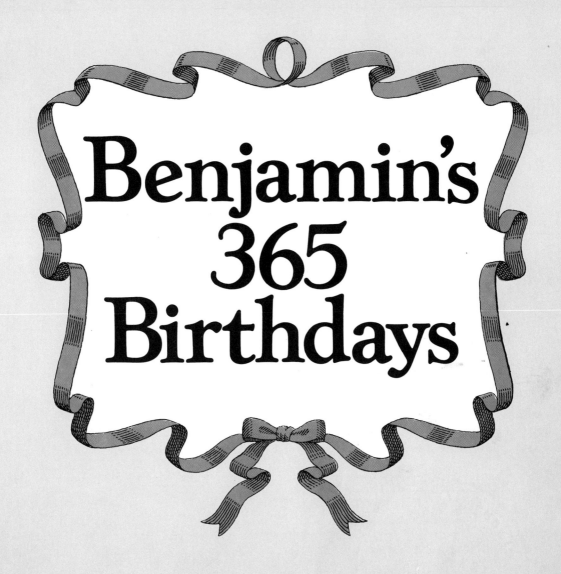

Benjamin's 365 Birthdays

Written by Judi Barrett and Drawn by Ron Barrett

Atheneum 1974 New York

Happy Birthday To You.

Benjamin had a birthday every April 6th.
Today was April 6th. So it was Benjamin's birthday again.
This year he was nine years old.

Benjamin was giving a lunch party for his friends.
They all arrived at noon and each of them brought him
a present.

He served grape jelly sandwiches, chocolate milk, straw-berry ice cream and cupcakes with candles.

Then he opened his presents.
They were really wonderful things.
Benjamin loved tearing off all the paper and ribbons
and finding what was inside.

A birdcage with a bird in it.

Marvelous yellow velvet trousers.

Roller skates.

A jigsaw puzzle.

And a model airplane.

He sat there, long after his friends had gone home,
looking at his presents and remembering how much fun it
had been opening them.

His birthday was over in a few hours, and it would be a
whole year, 365 days, before he had another one.
That made him sad.

Benjamin closed his eyes and tried to imagine what the birdcage had looked like all wrapped up, before he knew it was a birdcage. He tried to remember the excitement of opening it up.

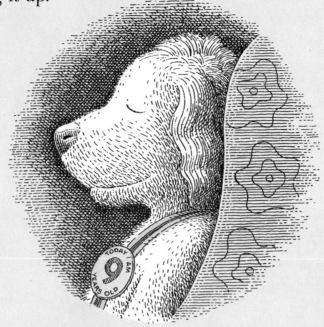

He realized that he could wrap the birdcage up again and pretend that he didn't know what it was. Then he could open it up the next morning like a brand new present.

So he wrapped it up.

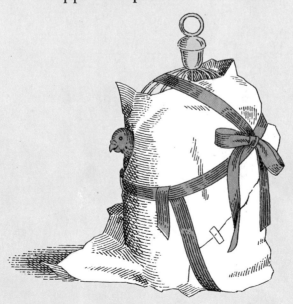

And then he went to sleep.

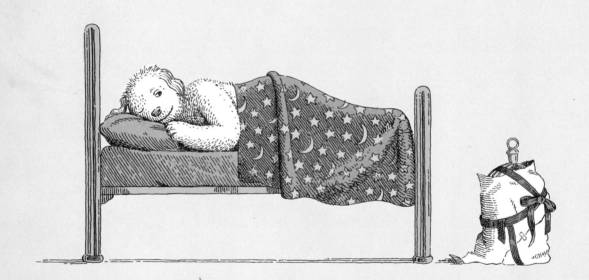

The next morning Benjamin woke up and there was the present.

He tore off the paper and ribbon and there was a birdcage with a bird in it. It was just like having another birthday.

That night he rewrapped another birthday present.

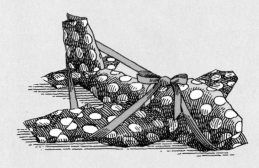

And the next morning he sort of had another birthday.

Each of the next three nights he rewrapped another present and opened it up the next morning.

Benjamin enjoyed having these extra birthdays. But now he had run out of birthday presents and he wondered what else he could wrap up and give to himself.

He looked all around the house, and that night he wrapped up his favorite suspenders.

In the morning he opened his present and found that it was his favorite suspenders. They had now become a birthday present, and Benjamin liked that.

It made his suspenders seem even nicer.

So every night Benjamin wrapped up something in his house.

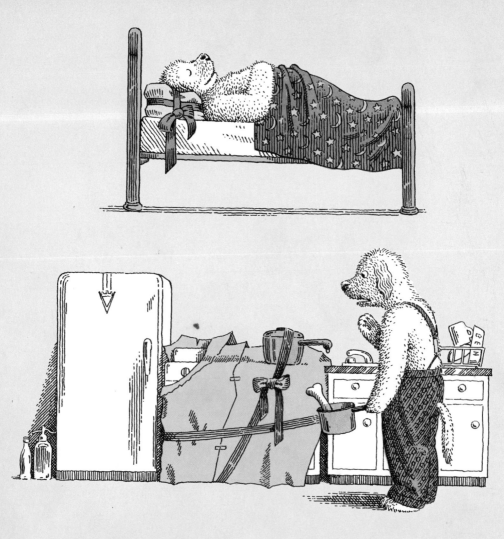

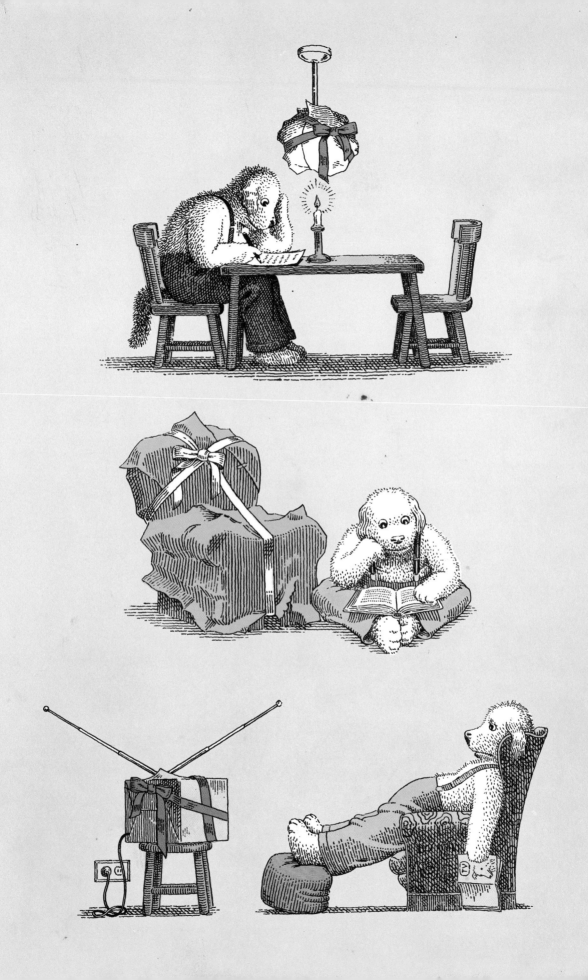

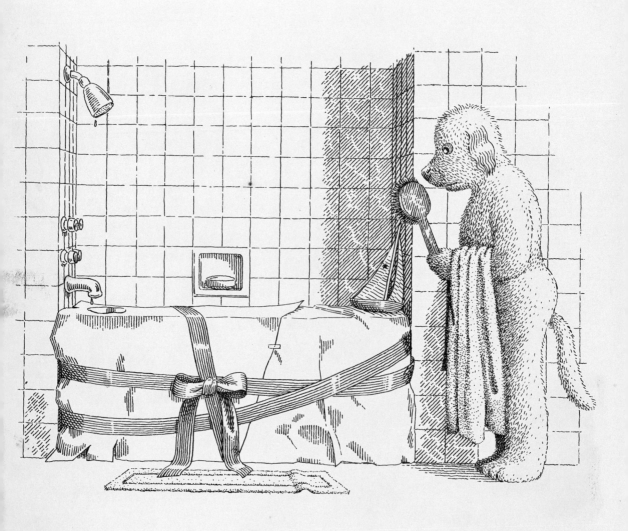

And he gave it to himself the next morning.

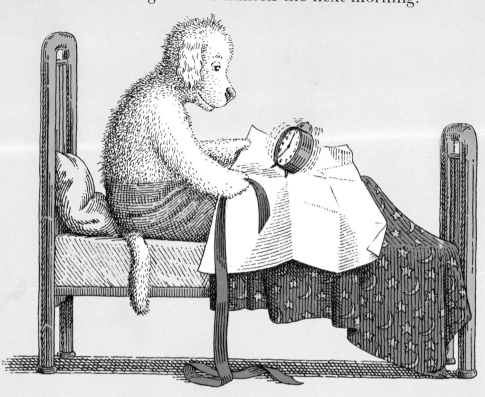

He did this every day of every month all year long, until
he had given himself everything in his house.

It added up to 365 birthdays. All Benjamin's.

And the 366th day was April 6th, Benjamin's real, genuine, honest-to-goodness ten year old birthday, and he was having a lunch party for his friends.

They arrived at noon, but Benjamin didn't seem to be home.

They looked all around,

under, and down,

and even up.

And there was Benjamin on his roof.

They couldn't imagine what he was doing up there.

Benjamin invited them to climb up the ladder.

There were cupcakes, ice cream and chocolate milk waiting for them. None of his friends had ever had a birthday party on a roof before.

They were confused by the big ribbon and the wrapping
paper above their heads.

They could not understand why Benjamin had tried to wrap up his house.

But Benjamin knew why he had done it, and it made him very happy.

Possibly the happiest he had ever been.

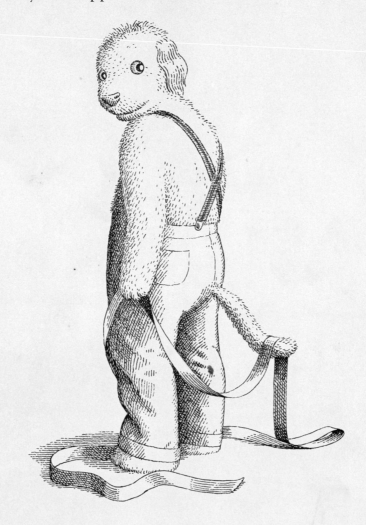

Now he had the world's largest and nicest birthday present.

Benjamin felt that he would never want another birthday present again, since everything around him was a present and always would be.